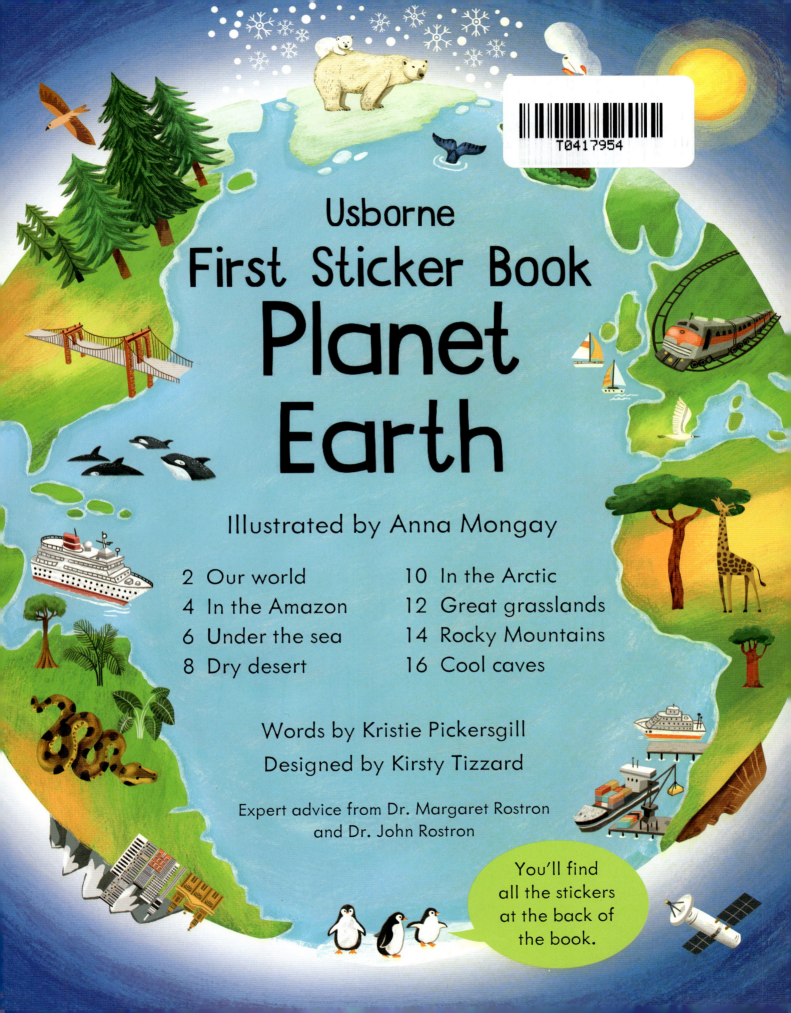

Usborne
First Sticker Book
Planet Earth

Illustrated by Anna Mongay

2 Our world
4 In the Amazon
6 Under the sea
8 Dry desert
10 In the Arctic
12 Great grasslands
14 Rocky Mountains
16 Cool caves

Words by Kristie Pickersgill
Designed by Kirsty Tizzard

Expert advice from Dr. Margaret Rostron
and Dr. John Rostron

You'll find all the stickers at the back of the book.

UNDER THE SEA

Over two thirds of our planet is covered by huge oceans and seas. Amazing creatures live under the waves, from tiny shrimp to giant squid.

Find another pelican diving for fish.

Fill this ledge with bright coral.

This looks like a good spot for an octopus.

Dry desert

Deserts are places where there is very little rain. They are often incredibly hot. This is part of the Sahara Desert. Many of the animals that live here come out at sunset when it's cooler.

Camels can go weeks without water, allowing them to travel across vast deserts. Stick a resting camel here.

Add an owl gliding through the air.

At an oasis, water from underground comes to the surface. Stick some wading flamingos in the water.

Stick on a desert fox coming out of its den.

9

In the Arctic

With freezing temperatures for much of the year, life is tough out on these islands in the Arctic. The animals that live here have thick fur or layers of fat to keep them warm.

Add some more houses in the snow.

Polar bears are strong swimmers. Find some to stick in the water.

A group of whales is called a pod. Find a pod of orcas to stick here.

Stick a narwhal in the cold water. Its tusk, or tooth, can grow to 3 m (10 ft) long.

Great grasslands

Grasslands are wide open spaces covered with lots of different grasses and small trees. On the Serengeti Plain in Africa, grass provides food for many animals.

Stick a sleepy leopard on the branch below.

Zebras are herbivores, which means they only eat plants. Add some zebras eating grass.

Rocky Mountains

In springtime, the snow on the Rocky Mountains melts and flows into the rivers. In the meadows below, bright wildflowers begin to bloom.

Mountain goats are excellent climbers. Stick some on this ledge.

Some animals go into a deep sleep, called hibernation, over winter. Add a bear just waking up.

Our world pages 2–3

Trans-Siberian Railway

Niagara Falls

Geyser

Northern Lights

The Himalayas

St. Basil's Cathedral

Great Barrier Reef

Typhoon

Serengeti Plain

Antarctic Research Station

Itsukushima Shrine

Volcano

COOL CAVES PAGE 16

Stalactites

Bats

Bridge

Abseiler

Scientists

Waterfall

Cavern

Divers

Stalagmites

Find spaces for these stickers anywhere in this book.